# Can We Go to the Moon and Back?

Mary Ellen Sherlock

*For my Mom*
*and for my grandmothers, my sisters, my*
*sister-in-laws, my nieces, my friends and all*
*those who have shown me the absolute and*
*unconditional love that mothers embody*

*XXOO*

"I can't wait for you
to be born, little one.
I already love you to
the moon and back"

"I am so lucky that I get to be your momma. I love you to the moon and back!"

"You are heaven sent and full of starlight my sweet Charlie. I love you to the moon and back!"

"....And the astronaut landed his spaceship back on earth and was cheered by all his family and friends. The End.
Alright Charlie, time for you to go to sleep"

"Wait, momma! Wait!
I want to go!
Can you take me there?"
"Where?" asked Momma
"To the moon and back!" said Charlie

" Oh my! The moon is very far away.!
Why do you want to go on such a
long trip?" Mom asked

"I want to go like you did momma
when you found out how much
you loved me!" said Charlie

" I DO love you, Charlie, to the moon and back!
Now, let me tuck you in....you need to get a good
night's sleep!
We will get to work on our adventure tomorrow."

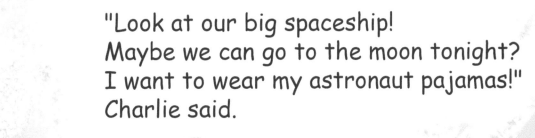

"Look at our big spaceship!
Maybe we can go to the moon tonight?
I want to wear my astronaut pajamas!"
Charlie said.

"Look at all those stars! There are so many.
Can you help me count them?" Mom asked.

"7, 8, 9, 10..."

Mom whispers as Charlie sleeps. "Outer space looks like night time but there are so many dif-ferent kinds of stars! Some of them shoot across the sky and others twinkle very brightly. There are swirly clouds of purple, pink and yellow.
I think those are planets in the distance. I see the moon coming up and the beautiful light of the sun. It is so quiet here Charlie."

"No matter where you are Charlie, my love for you will always be as bright as the stars, as powerful as a spaceship, as big as the universe, and as warm as the sun.

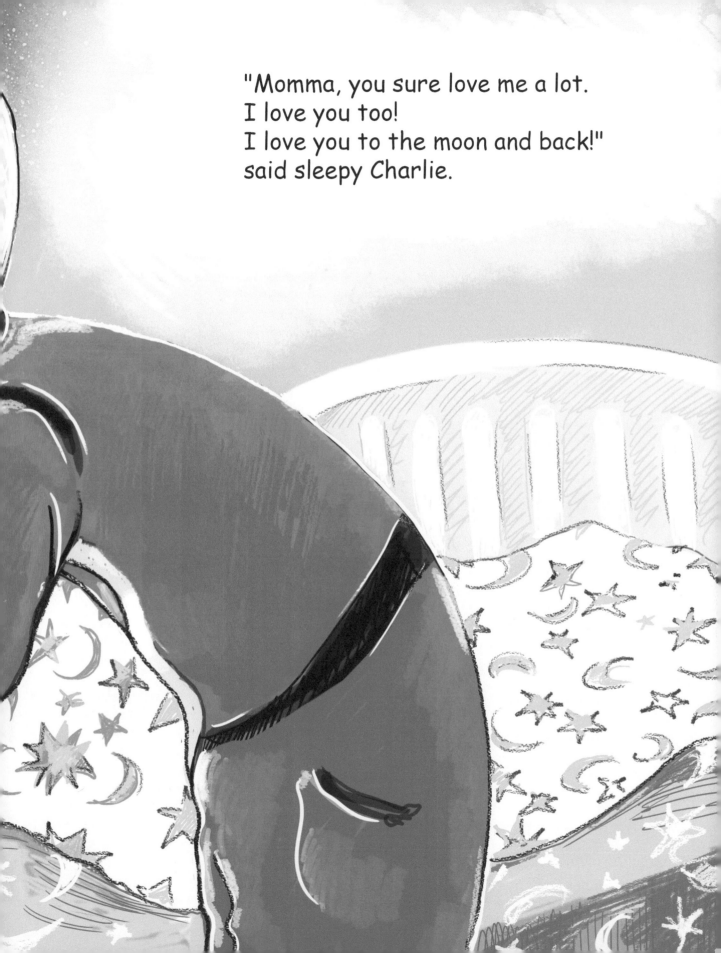

"Momma, you sure love me a lot.
I love you too!
I love you to the moon and back!"
said sleepy Charlie.

Lightning Source UK Ltd.
Milton Keynes UK
UKHW050818020621
384711UK00002BA/37